Christopher

HENRY

JAMES

PERCY

D1021946

TITLES AVAILABLE IN BUZZ BOOKS

First published 1990 by Buzz Books,
an imprint of the Octopus Publishing Group,
Michelin House, 81 Fulham Road, London SW3 6RB

LONDON MELBOURNE AUCKLAND

Copyright © William Heinemann Ltd 1990

All publishing rights: William Heinemann Ltd. All television
and merchandising rights licensed by William Heinemann Ltd
to Britt Allcroft (Thomas) Ltd exclusively, worldwide.

Photographs © Britt Allcroft (Thomas) Ltd 1985
Photographs by David Mitton and Kenny McArthur
for Britt Allcroft's production of Thomas the
Tank Engine and Friends.

ISBN 1 85591 001 2

Printed and bound in the UK

TOBY AND THE STOUT GENTLEMAN

buzz books

Toby is a tram engine. He is short and sturdy. He has cow-catchers and side-plates and doesn't look like a steam engine at all.

Toby's tramline runs alongside roads and through fields and villages. He takes trucks from farms and factories to the main line and he always rings his bell cheerfully to everyone he meets.

He has a coach called Henrietta who has seen better days. Toby is attached to Henrietta and always takes her with him.

"She might be useful one day," he said.

Henrietta used to have nine trucks rattling along behind her but now there are only three or four because the factories send their goods mostly by lorry.

The cars, buses and lorries often have accidents. Toby is always careful. He hasn't had an accident for years. But the buses are crowded and Henrietta is empty.

"I can't understand it!" says Toby, sadly.

People come to see Toby but they always laugh and stare.

"Isn't he quaint and old-fashioned!" they say. They make Toby so cross.

One day a lady and a stout gentleman with a little girl and boy stood nearby. The gentleman looked important but nice. He was, of course, the Fat Controller but Toby didn't know this yet.

"Come on, Grandfather!" called the children. "Do look at this engine."

"That's a tram engine, Stephen," said the stout gentleman.

"Is it electric?" asked Bridget.

"Whoosh!" hissed Toby, crossly.

"Sh! Sh!" said her brother. "You've offended him."

"But trams *are* electric, aren't they?" asked Bridget.

"They are mostly," said the stout gentleman, "but this is a steam tram."

"May we go in it, Grandfather?" asked the children.

The guard had begun to blow his whistle.

"Stop!" shouted the stout gentleman. He raised his arm and they all scrambled into Henrietta.

"Hip, hip, hurray!" chanted Henrietta as she rattled along behind Toby.

But Toby did not sing.

"Electric indeed!" he snorted. He was very hurt.

The stout gentleman and his family
climbed out at the next station.

"What's your name?" he asked.

"Toby, sir," said the tram engine.

"Thank you, Toby, for a very nice ride,"
said the stout gentleman.

16

"Thank *you*, sir!" said Toby, politely. He felt much better now. "This gentleman," he thought, "is a gentleman who knows how to speak to engines."

The children came every day for a fortnight to see Toby and Henrietta. Sometimes they rode with the guard and sometimes in the empty trucks.

On the last day of their holiday, the driver invited them into his cab.

Everyone was very sorry when the stout gentleman and his family had to go away.

"Goodbye," said Bridget and Stephen and they thanked Toby and his driver.

"Peep, pip, peep!" whistled Toby. "Come again, soon!"

"We will, we will!" cried the children and they waved until Toby was out of sight.

The months passed. Toby had few trucks to pull and even fewer passengers travelled on his tramline.

"This is our last day, Toby," said his driver, sadly, one morning. "The Manager says that we must close the line."

That day everyone wanted the chance of
a last ride with Toby and Henrietta.

Henrietta had more passengers than she
could manage. They rode in the trucks and
crowded into the brake van. The guard
didn't have enough tickets to go round!

As they travelled along, the passengers
joked and sang.

"Goodbye, Toby," said the passengers, afterwards. "We are very sorry that your line is closing down."

"So am I," said Toby, sadly.

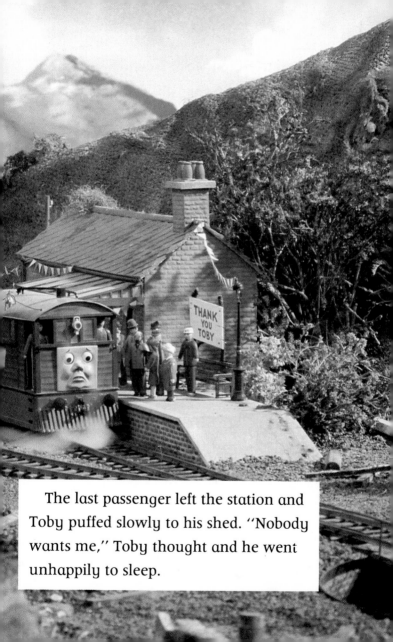

The last passenger left the station and Toby puffed slowly to his shed. "Nobody wants me," Toby thought and he went unhappily to sleep.

Next morning the shed doors were flung
open and Toby woke with a start. His driver
was waving a piece of paper.

"Wake up, Toby!" he shouted. "Listen to
this. It's a letter from the stout gentleman.
Toby listened and…

But I mustn't tell you any more or
I shall spoil the next story.

If you want to read the next story
it is called *Thomas in Trouble*

THOMAS

EDWARD

GORDON